PLEASE WASH
YOUR HANDS
BEFORE YOU READ ME
AND KEEP ME CLEAN

ENTERED

CAPTAIN TOAD
and the
MOTORBIKE

CAPTAIN TOAD
and the
MOTORBIKE

written and illustrated by

DAVID McPHAIL

A MARGARET K. MC ELDERRY BOOK

ATHENEUM   1981   NEW YORK

Library of Congress catalog card number: 78-59155
ISBN 0-689-50118-8
Copyright © 1978 by David McPhail
All rights reserved
Published simultaneously in Canada
by McClelland & Steward, Ltd.
Printed by Einson Freeman Graphics,
Fair Lawn, New Jersey
Bound by A. Horowitz & Son / Bookbinders
Fairfield, New Jersey
Designed by Marjorie Zaum
First Printing November 1978
Second Printing May 1981

For Mickey

Captain Toad was one of the best jumpers of all time. Even as a young toad he could jump higher and farther than any toad in his neighborhood. His fame spread, and jumpers came from far and wide to challenge him . . . but he never lost a single contest.

When finally there was no one left to jump against, he joined the Navy to see the world. Everywhere he went he gave friendly demonstrations of his remarkable jumping ability.

After a few years he was made captain of his own ship, and once, during a hurricane, he saved his entire crew by jumping ashore with a lifeline.

For his countless deeds of bravery Captain Toad
was awarded many medals which he wore proudly until
he retired from active service. At the retirement party

given in his honor he said, "I've had a wonderful and
exciting career, and now I look forward to some quiet
years in the country."

Captain Toad moved into a charming little cottage in the peaceful community of Basher's Hollow. There he spent most of his time tending his garden and reading books.

To keep his jumping legs in good condition, he bicycled five miles every day to the post office for his mail.

One Saturday morning while on his way home from the post office, Captain Toad was nearly run over by a speeding motorbike. It was the first of many that roared through the village that day in a cross-country race.

Anyone else would have been frightened by such a narrow escape, but not Captain Toad! "What a beautiful machine!" he said, and from that moment on he wanted more than anything in the world to drive a motorbike.

Every Saturday after that the motorbikes raced through Basher's Hollow. Captain Toad's friends and neighbors worried about the noise and the danger, but he looked forward to the races.

He tended his garden a little less, and read every book he could find about motorbikes. He tied a balloon to the frame of his bicycle, and when the spokes hit it they made a sound like a motor.

He padded his cap with rags and attached a pair of old welder's goggles to the brim. He took his old Navy coat out of his storage trunk and wore it all the time.

The citizens of Basher's Hollow – all but Captain Toad – sent a letter to the sponsors of the weekly race, demanding that the race be stopped. But the very next Saturday more bikes than ever showed up.

The citizens were furious. The time for action had come. They dug a deep, wide trench across the main road the night before the next race.

Captain Toad objected. "Someone might be hurt," he said, "even killed!"

No one paid him any attention, but to prevent him from trying to fill the trench, they sent a mole to guard him through the night.

Toward morning, the mole fell fast asleep. Captain Toad, dressed in his cap, goggles and Navy coat, climbed out through a window and headed for the trench.

He was almost there when he heard the first motorbike coming. It was the very same one that had nearly
run him over once before. Without hesitating even an
instant, Captain Toad hopped right out in front of the
racing motorbike and began waving his arms.

The driver had no time to stop.
He tried to swerve, but it was too late.
He was going to hit Captain Toad!

There was only one thing for Captain Toad to do. He jumped as high as he could—straight up in the air. But it was not quite high enough. Thwack! He collided with the bike driver's helmet. The driver was knocked off backwards and Captain Toad was sent spinning.

He did a triple somersault forward and came down
on the seat of the motorbike as it raced on toward the
gaping trench.

With Captain Toad holding on for dear life, the motorbike cleared the trench like a moon-bound rocket, landing on its rear wheel on the other side.

It raced on and on – through the finish line, the judges' table, and the winner's circle where the chief judge was waiting to award the winner's trophy.

The judge was caught up on the handle-bars of the motorbike and clung there until the bike ran into the river and sank into the mud.

Right there, the judge presented the trophy to Captain Toad who accepted it graciously. His dream had come true. He had ridden a motorbike, and he had even won a prize for doing it.

When the other motorbike drivers saw Captain Toad barely make it over the trench, they had turned around and left. "We're never coming back," they said. "This race course is too dangerous!"

Captain Toad was declared a hero by his friends and neighbors, and in his honor a big parade was held.

At the side of the road near the entrance to Basher's Hollow the grateful citizens set up Captain Toad's trophy with a sign that says:

Here lives Captain Toad
Who won the race
And saved this place.